EASY READERS

A NOTE TO PARENTS

Early Step into Reading Books are designed for preschoolers and kindergartners who are just getting ready to read. The words are easy, the type is big, and the stories are packed with rhyme, rhythm, and repetition.

We suggest that you read this book to your child the first few times, pointing to each word as you go. Soon your child will start saying the words with you. And before long, he or she will try to read the story alone. Don't be surprised if your child uses the pictures to figure out the text—that's what they're there for! The important thing is to develop your child's confidence—and to show your child that reading is fun.

When your child is ready to move on, try the rest of the steps in our Step into Reading series. **Step 1 Books** (preschool–grade 1) feature the same easy-to-read type as the Early Step into Reading Books, but with more words per page. **Step 2 Books** (grades 1–3) are both longer and slightly more difficult, while **Step 3 Books** (grades 2–3) introduce readers to paragraphs and fully developed plot lines. **Step 4 Books** (grades 2–4) offer exciting nonfiction for the increasingly independent reader.

The grade levels assigned to the five steps are intended only as guides. Some children move through all five steps very rapidly; others climb the steps over a period of several years. Either way, these books will help your child "step into reading" in style!

For my sister,
who likes to go to the ocean
–J. A.

Text copyright © 1997 by Jennifer Armstrong.
Illustrations copyright © 1997 by Lucia Washburn.
All rights reserved under International and Pan-American Copyright Conventions.
Published in the United States by Random House, Inc., New York, and
simultaneously in Canada by Random House of Canada Limited, Toronto.
http://www.randomhouse.com/

Library of Congress Cataloging-in-Publication Data
Armstrong, Jennifer. Sunshine, moonshine / by Jennifer Armstrong. p. cm.
— (Early step into reading) SUMMARY: Illustrations and rhyming text follow the
sun and moon as they shine on a young boy's day.
ISBN 0-679-86442-3 (pbk.) — ISBN 0-679-96442-8 (lib. bdg.)
[1. Sun—Fiction. 2. Moon—Fiction. 3. Stories in rhyme.] I. Title. II. Series.
PZ8.3.A63Su 1997 [E]—dc20 94-34992

Printed in the United States of America 10 9 8 7 6 5 4 3 2 1

STEP INTO READING is a registered trademark of Random House, Inc.

Early Step into Reading™

Sunshine, Moonshine

by Jennifer Armstrong
illustrated by Lucia Washburn

Random House 🏠 New York

Sun shines on the mountains.

Sun shines on the sea.

Sun shines on my pillow,
and says wake up to me.

Sun shines on a seashell.

Sun shines on a rock.

Sun shines on a crab,

and on a gull,

and on the dock.

Sun shines on the lighthouse.

15

Sun shines on a sail.

Sun shines as it sinks

into the ocean like a whale.

Moon shines as it rises.

Moon shines as I yawn.

Moon shines as I try to catch
the fireflies on the lawn.

Moon shines on the houses.

Moon shines on the cars.

Moon shines like a night-light
up among the stars.

Moon shines on the mountains.

Moon shines on the sea.

Moon shines on my pillow,
and says good night to me.